HOLLY KELLER
GRANDFATHER'S DREAM

Greenwillow Books, New York

For Nguyen thu Huong Norton Payson

and Nguyen Xuan Truong,

with admiration

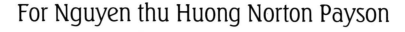

Watercolor paints and a black pen were used for the full-color art. The text type is Seagull.
Copyright © 1994 by Holly Keller. All rights reserved. No part of this book may be reproduced or utilized in any form
or by any means, electronic or mechanical, including photocopying, recording, or by any information storage and retrieval
system, without permission in writing from the Publisher, Greenwillow Books, a division of William Morrow
& Company, Inc., 1350 Avenue of the Americas, New York, NY 10019.   Printed in Singapore by Tien Wah Press
First Edition   10 9 8 7 6 5 4 3 2 1

Library of Congress Cataloging-in-Publication Data
Keller, Holly.
    Grandfather's dream / by Holly Keller.
            p.   cm.
    Summary: After the end of the war in Vietnam, a young boy's
grandfather dreams of restoring the wetlands of the Mekong delta,
hoping that the large cranes that once lived there will return.
    ISBN 0-688-12339-2 (trade).   ISBN 0-688-12340-6 (lib. bdg.)
    [1.Vietnam—Fiction.   2. Cranes (Birds)—Fiction.
3. Grandfathers—Fiction.]   I. Title.
PZ7.K28132Gr   1994   [E]—dc20
93-18186   CIP   AC

PROLOGUE

For as long as anyone can remember, the Plain of Reeds, in the Mekong delta in the country of Vietnam, was a large and beautiful wetland, where many birds, plants, and animals made their homes. The largest flying bird in the world, the Sarus crane, lived there and was treasured by the Vietnamese people as a symbol of long life and happy families.

During the Vietnam War several canals were dug across the wetland to drain the area. This damaged the vegetation that had been providing a good hiding place for soldiers. The canals also destroyed the natural flow of water in the Plain of Reeds, and the birds and animals could not continue to live there. Most of them disappeared or died. After the war much of that land was turned into rice fields.

Some of the older people remember the cranes, and would like to restore the wetland so that the birds can live there again. Most of the younger people would like to use the land to plant more rice. It is always hard to balance the traditions of the past and the needs of the future.

"The new dikes are built," Grandfather announced as he dropped a piece of fish into Nam's bowl.

"Will the cranes come back now?" Nam asked.

Grandfather sighed and took some rice. "We will see. Once there were so many that when they flew from the feeding ground at sunrise, they covered the whole winter sky. Then the war came, and when it was over, they were gone."

"Where did they go?"

"Safer places," Grandfather said, "and places where there was still plenty of food."

Mama poked the fire impatiently and turned over the last piece of fish. "Hurry and finish now, Nam," she said. "It's late. Your grandfather has made the whole village of Tam Nong worry about these birds that aren't good for anything!"

Papa patted Nam's hand. "When the rains come, the land inside the dikes will flood with water the way it always used to. The plants will grow again, and the cranes will come home."

"What if they don't?" Nam asked anxiously.

"If they don't," Papa said, putting down his bowl, "then the farmers will take back the land your grandfather and the others have reserved for the birds, and use it to plant more rice."

Grandfather shook his head. "And then all we will have are fat stomachs," he said angrily, and he got up from the table.

"It is past bedtime, Nam," said Mama.

Nam followed his grandfather out onto the back porch. He moved his sleeping mat close to where Grandfather was sitting, and his puppies, Cho-tom and Cho-phen, stretched out next to him.

"Grandfather," Nam asked, "why do you want the cranes to come back so much?"

"Because Vietnam was their home," the old man answered. "Cranes are strong birds and live long lives. We believed that they brought us good luck. Now the war is over, and we are all safe. The birds must be made safe, too, or they will be gone forever."

Grandfather sat for a long time without talking.

"Aren't you going to tell a story tonight?" Nam asked finally.

Grandfather smiled. "A short one," he said, "because it's late. In the old days," Grandfather began, "when there were still otters in the river, my father caught two young ones. He brought them home for me, and we fed them little pieces of cooked fish. Then my father and I trained them to catch live fish and bring them home."

"Why didn't they eat the fish they caught?" Nam asked.

Grandfather laughed. "Because we had taught them to eat only cooked fish, and they had forgotten that they were supposed to eat the live ones!"

Grandfather chuckled again as he remembered. "If the otters couldn't find a fish in the river, they would steal one. The women who were fixing dinner at the edge of the water were too busy talking to notice if a fish was snatched, and later they could never figure out what happened to their food!"

Nam fell asleep smiling, because the otter story was his favorite.

The monsoon began in the middle of May. The rain came down gently at first, and then in blinding sheets. The river swelled and the banks were flooded. The water stayed inside the dikes and did not drain off the land.

Nam spent most of his time in the house with the puppies, who were growing fast. Grandfather checked the dikes every morning, and then he sat patiently and watched the sky.

W hen the rains finally stopped, Grandfather got up early
every morning to look for the cranes. Mama always had
a bowl of steaming soup ready for him when he came home.

"Did you see any today?" Papa asked.

Grandfather shook his head. "But they will come, you'll see.
Last night I was sure I heard their call."

"You are living in the past," Mama said, and she frowned.
"Those birds are gone."

The days of the dry season were passing, and there was still no sign of the cranes. The village committee met and decided that if the birds did not come back before the next rainy season, the land in the reserve would be planted with rice.

Grandfather was very sad. "It was a silly dream," he said, and Nam felt sad, too.

A few weeks later Nam was in the fields watching the water buffalo. Cho-tom and Cho-phen came running across the field to play. Each dog had a small bird in its mouth.

Nam smiled. "Good dogs," he said, because he could see that the birds were not hurt.

When Nam got home, Grandfather was taking a nap.

"My dogs are just like your otters, Grandfather!" Nam called.

Grandfather opened his eyes. "Are they catching fish?"

"No," Nam said, and he laughed. "Birds, baby birds." Then Nam whispered to Papa, "The birds were gray and funny looking, and I have never seen that kind before."

Papa rubbed his chin thoughtfully, and then he put his finger across his mouth so Nam would know not to say anything.

The next morning Nam and Papa slipped out of the house before dawn. The village was dark and quiet. They reached the cranes' old feeding area just as the sun was beginning to rise. When Nam's eyes had adjusted to the pale light, he could see the cranes off in the distance.

"I have counted nearly two hundred!" Papa said.

"Can I tell Grandfather now?" Nam pleaded.

Papa nodded and pushed Nam off toward the village.

Nam couldn't get his feet to move fast enough. The sun was getting brighter, and he knew that the birds would soon be in the sky. "Come quickly, Grandfather," he shouted as he ran down the path.

He pulled Grandfather by the hand across the bridge and out toward the dikes.

In a few minutes more cranes than anyone could count flew over Tam Nong. The air was filled with their noisy call, and the whole village came out to see them.

Grandfather could hardly believe his eyes. "Aren't they beautiful!" he shouted happily.

And everyone agreed—even Mama.

That night when Nam was ready to go to bed, Grandfather sat down next to him.

"It was a good dream, after all," Nam said softly. "Do you think the cranes will stay now?"

"That is up to you," Grandfather said.

And Nam understood.